D1432224

This book is dedicated to my beloved son,
Quintarus K. Williams II.
Thank you for asking me questions
about being different and letting me see
the world through your eyes. You are
my inspiration and seeing the world
through your eyes is the most amazing
experience! You are a really special kid
and I love you tremendously!

To my husband Quin, thank you for our son and for always supporting my dreams, no matter what they may be. You are truly my soulmate and I love you!

To little Grace and my beautiful step children: Chelsey, Gavin, Jalen, Keegan, Hayden, and Sadie. Thank you for being such amazing kids and for adding so much laughter and love to my life. You are precious to me and I love you all so much.

To Nanna Patty, thank you for all the love, encouragement, and guidance you gave to me on this book! I love you!

I would like to thank Kelly Conley of @KellyConleyPhotography for the author photo. I hope you enjoy reading these books to baby Saige!

www.mascotbooks.com

The Adventures of Quintarus: Introducing My Big Biracial Family

For more information, please contact:
Mascot Books
620 Herndon Parkway, Suite 320
Herndon, VA 20170
info@mascotbooks.com

Library of Congress Control Number: 2020922902

CPSIA Code: PRT1120A
ISBN-13: 978-1-64543-627-0

Printed in the United States

THE ADVENTURES OF QUINTARUS

INTRODUCING MY BIG BIRACIAL FAMILY

Illustrated by Abira Das

Dr. Tracy Williams

My name is Quintarus
And I am extraordinary.
What do I mean?
Well, my name is not ordinary.

My name is quite long,
It comes from my dad.
We share the same name.
Mine is the one that he has.

I am quite special,
As you can see.
Neither one of my parents
Looks just like me!

My dad's skin is black.
My mom's skin is white.
I am part of both.
My skin is just right!

I am biracial.
Do you know what that means?
I am not black or white,
I am in between.

Did you know there are others
Who are both white and black?
Did you know they are animals
And some travel in packs?

They are exceptional!
I'll name just a few.

They are both
white and black,
just like me and you!

Penguins
and
pandas,

Kingsnakes and skunks,

Zebras and orcas,

Who would have thunk?

White tigers
and cows,

The giant
leopard moth,

Malayan Tapir,

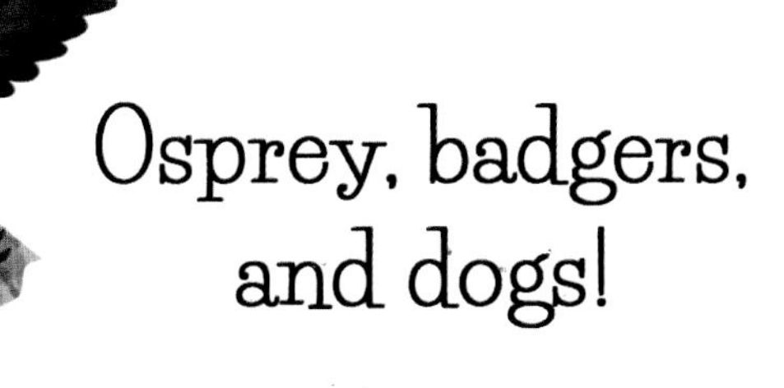

Osprey, badgers,
and dogs!

They are all different
But also the same.
They have the same colors
But different shapes and names.

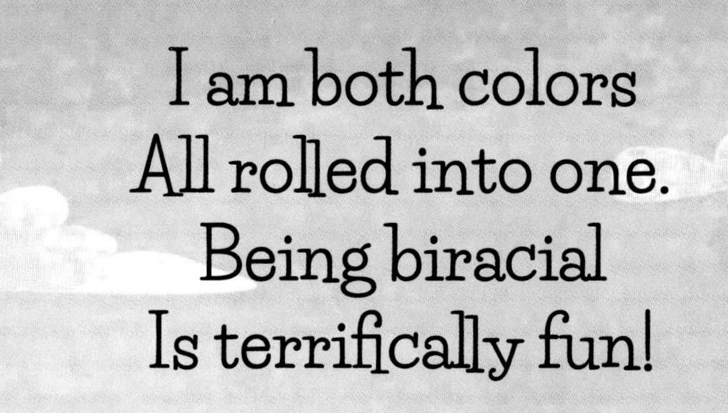

I am both colors
All rolled into one.
Being biracial
Is terrifically fun!

I'm a mixture of both
And that makes me complete.
That combination
Makes me unique!

My skin is light brown,
My eyes are brown too,
My hair is super curly,
Like many of you.

I play hide and seek
And games on the iPad.
I have fun playing sports
With my four brothers and my dad.

My three sisters look out for me.
Sometimes they are sweet,
Sometimes they annoy me
From my head to my feet.

My mom loves me to pieces,
We do things that are fun,
Like build forts or read books,
Go to the beach, and play in the sun.

My dad is the best dad.
He is kind, he is cool,
We watch basketball together,
We play in the pool.

From football to basketball,
Soccer, tennis, and track,

My parents stay busy,
And that is a fact.

We travel a lot,
See many new places
For my siblings' competitions,
Tournaments, and races.

To the world we are different
You may very well see.
It will not always be easy
Being you and being me.

Some people may see us
By the color of our skin
Or the way our hair curls
And we may not fit in.

Just make your own mark,
You just be you.
Because you can do anything.
That's what you can do!

So now that you know
A little more about me
I ask you to look in the mirror and see
How wonderfully perfect
And special you are.
That people will notice you
From near and from far.

Dr. Tracy Williams

obtained her Bachelor of Science degree in psychology (major) and history (minor) from Charleston Southern University and her Doctor of Pharmacy degree from the Medical University of South Carolina. She completed a pharmacy practice residency at Region One Medical Center (formerly known as The Med) in Memphis, Tennessee. It was here that she researched the use of unfractionated heparin in high-risk pregnancy, later published in the *Journal of Obstetric Medicine* (2016). After residency, she stayed on as the ER/shock trauma pharmacist at the Elvis Presley Memorial Trauma Center until meeting her husband and relocating to South Carolina. She presided over thirty-one pharmacies across South Carolina and Georgia for five years as their district manager until they were sold in June of 2020. She is currently employed by CVS Pharmacy in her hometown of Summerville as a pharmacy manager. In her spare time, she enjoys playing with her children, running marathons and half marathons, reading books, quilting, and gardening. She and her husband currently live in Summerville, South Carolina, with their eight children and two cocker spaniels.